WALT DISNEY'S
The JUNGLE BOOK

Random House New York

Library of Congress Cataloging in Publication Data
Walt Disney's, the jungle book. (Disney's wonderful world of reading, #20) The animal friends of the boy raised by wolves escort him out of the jungle to keep him safe from the tiger who seeks to kill him. [1. Jungle stories] I. Kipling, Rudyard, 1865-1935. The jungle book. II Title: The jungle book. PZ10.3.W18 [E] 74-3407. ISBN 0-394-82560-8. ISBN 0-394-92560-2 (lib. bdg.)
Manufactured in the United States of America

GROLIER
BOOK CLUB EDITION

Deep in the jungle Bagheera the panther
heard a strange sound.

It was the sound of someone crying.

He looked in the tall grass.

There was a baby boy!

Bagheera took the baby to a wolf family.
The little wolf cubs sniffed and sniffed.
"What kind of cub is this?" they asked.
"He is a boy cub," said Bagheera.
"We will call him Mowgli!" they said.

For ten years Mowgli lived with the wolves.
He learned to do everything the wolf cubs
could do.

He learned to walk.

He learned to scratch.

He even learned to lie down
and play dead.

Mowgli could also take a thorn out of
a wolf cub's paw.

That was something the wolf cubs could not do.

Bagheera watched Mowgli grow up.
He was very proud of him.

Shere Khan the tiger hid in the bushes
and watched Mowgli, too.

Long ago a hunter had shot at Shere Khan.
Now Shere Khan hated all men.

"As soon as that boy cub is alone,
I will get him," said the tiger.

"Then he cannot grow up to be a hunter."

Late one night the wolves met on Big Rock.

"Shere Khan wants Mowgli!" said one wolf.

"Mowgli is not safe with us any more,"
said another.

"But where will he go?" they wondered.

Then Bagheera spoke:

"I will take Mowgli to the man village.
He will be safe there."

That night Bagheera carried
Mowgli away.

Bagheera did not stop running
until they came to a big tree.

"We will sleep up there,"
said Bagheera.

"But I can't climb
such a big tree,"
said Mowgli.

Bagheera gave Mowgli a push.
"Up you go!" he said.

"I'm not sleepy yet,"
said Mowgli.
"Try to sleep anyway,"
said Bagheera.

Soon Bagheera was snoring.
Mowgli tried to sleep, too.

But they were not alone.
Kaa the snake was hiding in the tree.
Kaa pushed his head down through the leaves.
"Is that a juicy boy cub I see?" said Kaa.

Mowgli sat up.

"Go away, snake!" said Mowgli.
"I don't trust you."

"You can trust me," said Kaa.
"I am your friend."

Mowgli looked at Kaa.
Kaa looked at Mowgli.

Kaa's eyes stared
right into Mowgli's eyes.
Mowgli could not look away.
He was under Kaa's spell.
Kaa wrapped his long tail
around Mowgli.

"Now I have you!" said Kaa.
"What a juicy supper you will be!

Suddenly Bagheera woke up.
"Kaa!" he shouted.
"What are you doing?"
"Mind your own business!"
said Kaa.

"Mowgli IS my business!"
said Bagheera.

He slapped Kaa —WHACK!—
right down to the ground.

Kaa landed with a thud and wiggled away.
"Ouch!" he said. "You bent my tail!"

Then Bagheera said to Mowgli:

"Kaa the snake tried to get you.

Shere Khan the tiger wants to get you, too.

You are not safe in the jungle.

You must go live in the man village."

"I want to live in the jungle!" cried Mowgli.

Mowgli ran out on a log by the river.

Bagheera went after him.

Mowgli grabbed hold of a branch.

Bagheera grabbed hold of Mowgli.

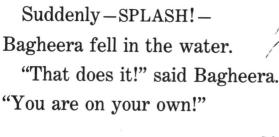

Suddenly—SPLASH!—

Bagheera fell in the water.

"That does it!" said Bagheera.

"You are on your own!"

Mowgli walked away
from Bagheera.
"I don't need him!" he said.
But after a while he felt lonely.

Then Mowgli heard
a happy song:
"Dooby dooby doo,
dooby dooby dee,
The life of a bear
is the life for me."

It was a big, happy, singing bear.

"Hi, I'm Baloo," said the bear.

"Who are you?"

"My name is Mowgli," said the boy.

"Are you all alone?" asked Baloo.

"I was," said Mowgli. "But now I'm with you.
Will you show me how to live like a bear?"

"Sure," said Baloo.
"Just do what I do."
So Mowgli learned
to walk like a bear.

He learned to growl
like a bear.

He even learned to fight
like a bear.

"How am I doing?"
asked Mowgli.

"You will make a great bear,"
said Baloo.

Mowgli and Baloo floated down the river.
Baloo was singing his song:
"Dooby dooby doo, dooby dooby dee,
The life of a bear is the life for me."

"I like being a bear," said Mowgli.

Up in the trees the monkeys were chattering.

But Mowgli and Baloo did not see them.

Suddenly the monkeys
grabbed Mowgli.
They wanted to play with hi

"Leave him alone!"
shouted Baloo.
But the monkeys
just laughed.

The monkeys
swung Mowgli
from tree to tree.

They were having fun.
"Put me down!"
cried Mowgli.

But the monkeys just laughed some more.

At last they swung Mowgli down
in front of their king.

"King Louie!" they cried.
"Look at what we found."

King Louie scratched his head and said:

"He looks a little like a monkey."

"I'm a boy cub!" said Mowgli.

The king popped a banana in Mowgli's mouth.
"Now you are a monkey," said Louie

Louie picked Mowgli up
and swung him around.
Mowgli began to feel a little dizzy.

"Let's have a party," the monkeys cried.
Everybody started dancing.
A big monkey came to the party.
It was Baloo, dressed up like a monkey.
Baloo grabbed Louie.
He swung him around and around.
Louie began to feel a little dizzy.

Then Baloo grabbed Mowgli.

They danced right out
of the monkey party.
Nobody saw them go.

The two friends sat down to rest.

"I am glad you came, Baloo," said Mowgli.
"They wanted to make a monkey out of me.
But I'm going to be a bear."

"No," said Baloo. "You are a boy!
You belong in the man village."

"That is what Bagheera said," cried Mowgli.
"But I won't live in the man village.
I want to stay in the jungle."
So Mowgli ran away from Baloo, too.
But a storm was coming.
The jungle was getting darker.

Suddenly a tiger leaped out of the bushes.

"A boy cub alone in the jungle!" he roared.

"Who are you?" asked Mowgli.

"I am the great Shere Khan," said the tiger.
"You can't get away from me!"

"I am not afraid of you," said Mowgli.

"You must be afraid of me," said Shere Khan. "Everyone is afraid of me."

"Well, I'm not!" said Mowgli.

"Look!" said the tiger. "I will count to ten. You must try to get away."

Shere Khan began to count.

"One, two, three, four. . . ."

Just then lightning flashed in the sky.
It crashed through the trees.
Shere Khan stopped counting.
He let out a terrible roar.
Full of fear, he raced away.

The great Shere Khan was afraid of lightning!

Baloo and Bagheera came running up to Mowgli.
"We heard Shere Khan roar," said Baloo.
"Where is he?"

"The storm scared him away," said Mowgli.
"But he will be back," said Bagheera.
"Come with us. We will take you to the man village."

Outside the man village a girl was
getting water at the river.

"That is a girl cub," said Bagheera.

"She is a lot like me," said Mowgli.

"Maybe I will live here for a while."

So Mowgli went into the village
with the girl.

After all, he was not a wolf cub.

He was not a bear or a monkey.

He was a boy.

And he belonged with other boys and girls.

"I think Mowgli will stay in the man village," said Bagheera.

"Yes," said Baloo. "But I still think he would have made a great bear."